Precious 2 Princess

Starry Night On the Beach

Rebecca Parkinson

CWR

On the Beach

Grandad always said that Daisy was his pretty, precious princess. That's why he gave her a special present.

'Daisy,' he said, 'precious princesses should learn precious secrets. This book will teach you many of the things you need to know as you grow up in this world. Read it well.'

It was then that the adventures began …

Daisy skipped happily along the beach, enjoying the feel of the warm grainy sand between her toes. It had been such a beautiful morning! She always loved being on holiday, but this year they were staying in a caravan so close to the beach that they would be able to play there every day!

Daisy jingled the coins she was clutching tightly in her hand. She was so glad that Grandma had given her some holiday money to spend. She had seen just what she wanted to buy.

She turned to wave at Mum who was following close behind her, holding tightly onto Jack's hand. He had just learnt to walk and was desperate to escape from her so he could run into the sea.

Daisy stopped outside the small, brightly-coloured beach shop and glanced at the blow-up boats, fishing nets and windmills lined up outside the door. Then she hurried inside and walked slowly across the shop. To her relief the pink and silver stripy bucket and spade were still there on the shelf.

'Please can I buy those?' Daisy asked the lady behind the counter.

The lady smiled and lifted them down.

'These are the last two,' she said. 'I think if you had been a few minutes later you could have been very disappointed.'

Daisy sighed with relief and quickly gave the lady her money.

As she left the shop Daisy saw a little girl and her dad walking towards her. She could hear the little girl's voice clearly over the sound of the sea.

'So Dad, they're on a shelf and they're all pink and silvery and the best bucket and spade I've *ever* seen!'

Daisy saw her mum glance at her but she kept on walking, pretending that she hadn't heard.

After a while Daisy saw the little girl and her dad walk back along the beach and sit down a short distance away. The girl was carrying a new green bucket and spade but it was easy to see that she had been crying. Daisy turned away and pretended to be busy building a sandcastle.

Daisy tried hard to get rid of the sad feeling deep down inside her, but it was no use. She felt rather cross. Today had started off as such an exciting day and she couldn't really understand why she felt so bad. Eventually she asked Mum if they could go back to the caravan and wait for Dad to return from shopping in the local town.

Once inside the caravan Daisy went into her room, shut the door and sat down on her bed. She was glad she had brought Grandad's special book on holiday with her. It had helped her in the past; maybe it could help her again today. Slowly she opened the book and began to read …

Suddenly the room began to spin. Daisy felt tingles running through her body. She could hear gentle music. She shut her eyes tight. This had happened before … Where would she end up this time?

When Daisy opened her eyes she was standing on a hill at the front of a large crowd of people. She was wearing a long dress that reached down to her ankles and she had sandals on her feet. No one saw her arrive; everyone's eyes were firmly fixed on a man who was speaking to them.

Almost immediately the man finished what He was saying and what appeared to be a group of friends walked over to Him. Daisy was close enough to hear what they said.

'Jesus, You've been speaking all day. These crowds must be so hungry! Don't you think You should send them away so they can get some food?'

Jesus shook His head. 'Why don't you feed them?' He asked. 'Then they won't need to go away.'

The friends started to giggle.

'It would take so much money to buy all these people food,' they laughed. 'There must be at least 5,000 men here, never mind the women and children! There's no way we could ever afford to feed them all!'

It was then that Daisy noticed a small boy standing by the side of her. He was very quiet and he was looking intently into a small bag he was holding. As Daisy watched he wandered slowly over to the group of men and tapped one of them on the back.

'Excuse me,' he asked politely. 'I wondered if Jesus would like this.'

He held out the bag.

The man took the bag and pulled out two small fish and five small rolls of bread. He was smiling as he showed them to Jesus; but Jesus didn't laugh. Daisy couldn't hear what Jesus said but she saw the look in His eyes as He thanked the boy. Daisy knew that something special was going to happen.

The boy went back to stand next to Daisy.

'Aren't you hungry?' she asked him shyly.

The boy nodded his head. 'I'm starving!' he answered. 'But I thought Jesus might need it more than me.'

Jesus asked His friends to get everyone to sit down on the grass. Then, to Daisy's amazement, He held the bread and fish up in the air and thanked God for them!

'Hand it round,' He said to His surprised friends.

Daisy was glad that she was near the front. She was hungry and it was obvious this small amount of food would not go far. But she was wrong! The bread and fish were passed from person to person until everyone in the crowd had eaten so much they were completely full-up.

The little boy nudged Daisy.

'Is that really my dinner?' he asked in a confused voice.

Daisy nodded.

'Wow!' said the little boy. 'I'd heard that Jesus could do anything, but that was amazing!'

As the leftovers of food were collected up in baskets Daisy saw Jesus look over at the little boy again and smile. It was a smile that said how proud He was of the boy and how happy He was with what the boy had just done. The boy smiled back and Daisy knew he was very glad that he had been willing to share his lunch.

Suddenly Daisy felt tingles running through her body. She could hear gentle music again and things began to spin. She shut her eyes tight …

When Daisy opened her eyes she was back sitting on her bed with Grandad's book resting on her knee. She knew what she had to do. The little boy had shared his dinner even though he was very hungry and Jesus had been pleased and done something amazing with it. She knew she needed to share too.

'That's very kind of you,' the little girl's dad said. 'Are you really sure?'

Daisy turned and saw the look on Mum's face. It was the same look that she had seen on Jesus' face earlier that day. She knew she had made her mum very proud.

'I'm certain,' she said giving a watery smile.

As they walked slowly back to the caravan a car pulled up alongside and Dad jumped out.

'You look a bit miserable love,' he said. 'I think I might have something in here to cheer you up. I just saw it in a shop in town and thought of you!'

Dad opened the boot and pulled something out.

Daisy and Mum both gasped and then started to laugh.

In Dad's hand was a pink and silver stripy bucket and spade. Now it was Daisy's turn to throw her arms round Dad.

Suddenly this was becoming the best day ever!

Why not read this story in your own Bible? You will find it in Bible book John, chapter 6 verses 1 to 13.

$\mathcal{S}$tarry $\mathcal{N}$ight

Grandad always said that Daisy was his pretty, precious princess. That's why he gave her a special present.

'Daisy,' he said. 'Precious princesses should learn precious secrets. This book will teach you many of the things you need to know as you grow up in this world. Read it well.'

It was then that the adventures began …

Daisy snuggled down under her warm duvet and listened to Mum's footsteps going quietly downstairs. It had been such a beautiful birthday! She lifted her head to look at the pile of presents beside her bed. People had bought her some lovely things; she could hardly wait to play with them all in the morning!

Daisy gazed across the room to her mirror, around which Mum had draped the long string of tiny star lights which her best friend Katie had given to her. The stars looked so realistic, glowing softly in the darkness.

A smile spread across Daisy's face as she remembered her walk with Dad the previous evening. Holding tightly to her hand, Dad had led her into the middle of a field where he stopped and pointed up into the night sky. Daisy had never seen anything so beautiful! The moon shone so brightly that it almost hurt her eyes, and in the blackness of the sky millions of stars twinkled like precious jewels. Daisy wondered if she could see the same sight again tonight.

She climbed out of bed and tiptoed softly over to the window. She made a tiny crack in the curtains and peered up excitedly into the sky. She was disappointed. There were no glistening stars, just dull, grey clouds that even blocked out the moonlight.

It felt cold! Daisy shivered and hurried back to bed. She could hear the wind blowing through the trees outside and she felt glad that her mum allowed her to keep the star lights on while she fell asleep. She closed her eyes and slowly drifted off into a lovely dream.

Suddenly Daisy shot upright in bed. Her room was dark. She was frightened. Outside the wind was howling through the trees and a loud crash of thunder made her jump.

'It's only a storm,' she whimpered to herself. 'It will be over soon.'

Daisy waited but the storm didn't stop. Instead the wind seemed to get stronger and the thunder seemed to get louder. Suddenly a bright flash of lightning lit up the room and Daisy began to cry. She wanted to go and get Mum but she was too scared to get out of bed and she didn't want to shout in case she woke up baby Jack. She reached out and flicked on her bedside lamp.

By the light of her lamp Daisy saw Grandad's special book lying on the bedside table. Grandad always said it would help her as she grew up. She needed some help now! Slowly she opened the book and began to read …

Suddenly the room began to spin. Despite feeling frightened Daisy felt tingles running through her body. She could hear gentle music. She shut her eyes tight. This had happened before … where would she end up this time?

When Daisy opened her eyes she was wearing a long dress and she could feel grains of sand between the toes of her bare feet. She was sitting on a wooden floor and there was a large cover draped over her, with a small slot in it through which she could see. Peeping out, she was relieved to find that it was a warm, sunny day.

Daisy jumped as she heard a man's voice close by.

'Let's go over to the other side of the lake,' the voice said, and suddenly the floor where she was sitting began to rock.

'OK, Jesus,' answered a different voice. 'But You look tired. Why not see if You can get a bit of sleep?'

Suddenly Daisy realised where she was.

'I'm in a boat …' she whispered to herself, '… and we're about to set sail!'

As Daisy watched, a group of men climbed aboard and another man pushed the boat gently away from the shore. Most of them began to row, but one man moved towards the back of the boat, cuddled down on a cushion and in a few seconds was fast asleep.

'Jesus is asleep already,' she heard someone whisper.

'Good,' said another voice quietly. 'He's been helping crowds of people for days and days. He needs a rest.'

Daisy liked the feel of the boat gently bobbing along in the water. Through the slot she could see the clear, blue sky and hear the men talking in quiet voices. She could understand how Jesus could fall asleep so easily; everything was warm, peaceful and calm.

Then suddenly, without warning, everything changed!

Thick black clouds appeared in the sky. The boat began to sway from side to side. The men's voices became louder and they sounded worried.

'This storm looks like a bad one,' someone shouted.

'Didn't see it coming!' another voice answered. 'We'll have to keep rowing. We're in the middle of the lake. We need to get to the other side.'

Under her cover Daisy began to feel frightened. The wind was now howling round the boat which seemed to be rocking violently from side to side. Daisy clung on, hoping they wouldn't tip over. Through the slot she could see water sloshing in the bottom of the boat and the men trying frantically to bale it back into the lake. She could tell that even the men were becoming scared. She wanted to go home.

'We're not going to make it!' bellowed a voice above the noise of the storm. 'This is too strong for us. I've never seen anything like it!'

Daisy jumped as another man leapt into the back of the boat and began to shake Jesus, who was still sleeping peacefully.

'Jesus! Jesus!' he shouted. 'Wake up! Don't You care that we're all going to drown?'

Jesus rubbed His eyes and sat up. Daisy was surprised that His face was calm. He didn't seem worried or frightened in any way. He stood up slowly and looked out over the wildly tossing waves.

Then Daisy heard His voice speaking clearly above the howling of the wind.

'Quiet!' He said simply. 'Be still!'

At once the wind dropped. The waves became calm and the sun began to appear from behind the clouds.

Jesus sat down again. All the men were gazing at Him. Daisy kept her eyes fixed on His face. She could hardly believe what she had just seen.

'Why were you afraid?' Jesus asked the men. 'Do you still not really believe I can take care of you?'

No one answered but Daisy saw the look in Jesus' eyes. She thought He looked hurt, as if what He wanted more than anything was for His friends to trust Him to care for them.

Suddenly Daisy felt tingles running through her body. She could hear gentle music again and things began to spin. She shut her eyes tight …

When Daisy opened her eyes she was sitting back in her bed with Grandad's book resting on her knee. The wind was still howling outside but she smiled. Suddenly it was all clear. She had no need to be frightened. Jesus was stronger than the wind and the waves. He had taken care of His friends in the storm and He would take care of her now.

The bedroom door opened and Mum walked in.

'Are you all right, love?' Mum asked softly. 'I woke up and thought you might be frightened.'

Daisy smiled. 'I was a bit,' she admitted, as Mum sat down on the edge of the bed. 'But I'm not any more.'

'Good,' said Mum. 'But remember I'm always here if you need me.'

Mum gave Daisy a big hug and stroked her head gently as she lay down. She kissed her forehead and flicked off the light.

'Goodnight,' she whispered, tiptoeing out of the room.

'Night,' Daisy murmured, sighing happily. She knew now that Jesus was always there to care for her, but it was still nice to have someone to hug!

Why not read this story in your own Bible? You will find it in Bible book Mark, chapter 4 verses 35 to 41.

On the Beach + Starry Night

For Anna.
Thank you x

OTHER TITLES IN THIS SERIES INCLUDE:

Harry's Hideout: Spot the Difference/Big Splash
Harry's Hideout: Glorious Mud/Mini-beasts
Precious Princess: Ballerina Necklace/The Birthday Present

Copyright text © Rebecca Parkinson 2013
Copyright illustrations © CWR 2013

Published 2013 by CWR, Waverley Abbey House, Waverley Lane, Farnham, Surrey GU9 8EP, UK. CWR is a Registered Charity – Number 294387 and a Limited Company registered in England – Registration Number 1990308.

The right of Rebecca Parkinson to be identified as the author of this work has been asserted by her in accordance with the Copyright, Designs and Patents Act 1988.

Visit www.cwr.org.uk/distributors for a list of National Distributors.
Concept development, editing, design and production by CWR.
Illustrations by Mike Henson at CWR
Printed in China by 1010 Printing International
ISBN: 978-1-78259-055-2